SURFING THREE-SIXTY

Jane West

Illustrated by Robin Lawrie

Titles in First Flight Level 2

Car Boot Genie

Monster Cards

Shhh! My Family Are Spies

Ghost Dog Mystery

Chip Boy

Sky Bikers

Surfing Three-Sixty

Something in the Kitchen

The Ghost in the Art Room

Robert and the Werewolf

The Biggest Lies Ever

Mad about Money

Badger Publishing Limited
Oldmeadow Road, Hardwick Industrial Estate,
King's Lynn PE30 4JJ
Telephone: 01438 791037

www.badgerlearning.co.uk

Surfing Three-Sixty ISBN 978 1 84424 841 4

First edition © 2006
This second edition © 2014

Text © Jane West 2006
Complete work © Badger Publishing Limited 2006

Series Editor: Jonny Zucker
Publisher: David Jamieson
Commissioning Editor: Carrie Lewis
Editor: Paul Martin
Design: Fiona Grant
Illustration: Robin Lawrie

SURFING THREE-SIXTY

Jane West

Contents

Stranger on the beach

Jake looked at the sea.
He hated it.
He hated the grey waves and he hated
the beach.
He had been happy at his old school.
Then his dad left, and everything
changed.

"We'll live by the sea with your
grandparents," said Jake's mum.
Her mouth smiled, but she looked sad.

So they had moved house. And now Jake didn't have any friends.

The wind was cold. Jake felt drops from the waves on his cheeks.

Suddenly, Jake heard a voice. "What is wrong with you?"

5

Jake looked round. It was an older boy. "I'm fine," he said.

The boy smiled. "I'm glad I'm not as 'fine' as you. You going in?"

It was a strange question. There was nowhere to go 'in'.

"The sea. Are you going boarding – you know – for a surf?"

Jake said no. He didn't want to say he couldn't surf. He turned his back. He wanted the boy to go away.

"I can teach you – if you want to learn,"
said the boy.

Jake turned round. "Really?
You'll teach me?"

"Yes!" said the boy. "Why not? I'm Sully.
You can have this wetsuit," said Sully,
"and I've got an old bodyboard you
can have."

Jake got into the wetsuit and Sully
zipped it up. It was hard to breathe.
Sully said it had to be tight to stop
the water getting in.

The bodyboard was made of foam
and plastic.

Sully tied it to his wrist with elastic
to stop it getting lost in the sea.

The waves looked much bigger now.
But Jake didn't want to show
that he was afraid.

"I'm ready," he said.

"We will take it easy today," said Sully.
"You have to learn which waves are best."

The sea was cold. Jake held
the bodyboard in front of him.

"Face the beach," shouted Sully
over the noise of the waves.
"When I say JUMP, jump onto the
wave and let it carry you in."

Then Sully yelled, "JUMP!"
and Jake jumped.

The wave raced up the beach with Jake
on top. It was brilliant.

Sully waved. "You're a surfer now!"

Jake went to the beach every day.
Sully was always there. He showed Jake
lots of moves.

It was the best time Jake had ever had.

School was okay, too. Jake made some friends. He told them about bodyboarding.

"There's a competition in a few weeks," said his friend Alex.

"Why don't you go for it? The prize is a new wetsuit."

Jake could not wait to tell Sully about it.

But Sully didn't think the competition was a good idea. For him the sea was a place to think. He did not surf for competitions.

"But the prize is a new wetsuit," said Jake.

"Look at the sea," said Sully. "Being on the sea is about finding out who you are. It is not about competitions."

Jake was angry. "Well, I'm going to do it anyway. I need a new wetsuit."

Sully didn't say anything, but he looked sad. Jake felt sorry.

"Okay, if you don't like it, I won't do it," said Jake.

"Come on. You can teach me that new move!"

Sully smiled. "Okay. Are you ready for a three-sixty?"

A three-sixty was when you spun in a circle on your board. It was hard.

"I'm ready!" said Jake.

It took weeks to learn the three-sixty.

One day Jake stayed in the sea so long that it was dark when he came home.

"Your tea is cold," said Jake's mum, crossly. "Where have you been?"

"Surfing," said Jake.

"…and you've got homework to do," she went on.

Jake ate his tea while his mum shouted. He didn't listen. He was too happy. At last he could do it – he could do a three-sixty.

Jake couldn't wait to tell Alex at school the next day.

"Cool!" said Alex. "How did you learn to do a three-sixty?"

"This boy Sully has been teaching me," said Jake. "Do you know him?"

"Yes," said Alex. "He left school and he hasn't got a job. He just lives at the beach all the time. Really sad."

Jake had thought Sully was cool. He didn't like to hear bad things about him. But he wanted to be friends with Alex, too.

"Are you doing that surfing competition?" asked Alex. "Go on! I'll put your name down."

"Ok," said Jake. "I need a new wetsuit."

Jake didn't go to the beach that day.
He went to Alex's house and listened
to music.

The next day Jake saw Sully on the beach.
"I will do that surfing competition,"
said Jake. "I think I could win."

Sully looked sad. "You said you were not
going to."

"No!" said Jake. "You told me not to.
But I don't have to listen to you."
He turned his back on Sully and
walked away.

Later, he felt bad about what he'd said to Sully.

"I'll tell him I'm sorry," he said to himself. "It will be ok."

But Sully was not at the beach the next day, or the day after that. It was no fun surfing by himself.

Jake missed Sully.

Competition

As the competition got nearer,
Jake was worried.

"What if I mess up?" he said. "What if
I fall off? What if I can't do it?"

On the day of the competition,
the sun was shining. The sea looked
clear and blue.

A lot of people had come to watch.
Jake went to the competitors' ring.

He felt a mess in his old wetsuit
and borrowed board.

The other surfers looked older
and bigger. Jake wanted to back out.

Jake's name was called. He took his
time. He had four waves to show
his best moves.

Jake took off on his first wave, making
two nice turns.

Then he did well on the second and third waves, making some more brilliant moves.

Jake heard the crowd cheer.

"One more wave," said Jake.

The fourth wave was huge. It came at him like a truck.

It was time to do the new move –
the three-sixty. Jake waited, then
jumped onto the board at
the right moment.

He pulled the side of his bodyboard.
The bodyboard spun round.

The crowd started to clap. He had
done it! He had done the three-sixty.

But suddenly the bodyboard slipped
and Jake was in the water.

A wave crashed on top of him.
Then another, and another.

Jake was too tired to swim any more...

Jake woke up on the beach, with his mother looking down at him.
Her eyes were scared.

"Oh Jake, I thought you were going to drown!"

"That would never happen," said another voice.

"Sully!" gasped Jake.

"You're lucky we've got such good lifeguards," said Jake's mum.

"You're a lifeguard?" asked Jake.

"Yeah. Best job in the world," said Sully. "Besides, you needed a mate to watch your back."

"Did I win?" asked Jake.

"No," said Sully. "If you hadn't fallen off, I think you could have. Sorry."

"Never mind," said Jake. "I'm glad we are still mates."

A voice came over the loud speakers, "And the best wipe-out of the day goes to … Jake Rivers!"

Jake stared. "I won something?"

"Yeah," laughed Sully. "You got the prize for the hairiest wipe-out in history! You got the prize for falling off!"

Jake laughed out loud.

"Cool!" he said.